First published in the United States, Great Britain, Canada, Australia, and New Zealand in 1998,
2014 by NorthSouth Books, Inc., an imprint of NordSüd Verlag AG, CH-8005 Zürich, Switzerland.

Distributed in the United States by NorthSouth Books, Inc., New York 10016.
Library of Congress Cataloging-in-Publication Data is available.
ISBN: 978-0-7358-4186-4 (trade edition)
1 3 5 7 9 • 10 8 6 4 2
Printed in Germany by Grafisches Centrum Cuno GmbH & Co. KG, Calbe, July 2014.
www.northsouth.com

FSC
www.fsc.org
MIX
Paper from
responsible sources
FSC® C043106

Brigitte Weninger
Eve Tharlet

Merry Christmas, Davy!

North South

Christmas was coming. The woods were buried under a thick blanket of snow, but the Rabbit family was safe and warm inside their burrow. Father Rabbit had just finished telling the children all about Santa Claus.

"Now, what does Santa Claus like us to do?" he asked them gently.

"He likes us to be good," said Davy.

"And to help one another," said Manni.

"And to share things!" added Lina.

"And to be kind and loving," said big brother Max.

"I see you have all been paying attention," said Father, laughing. "And now off to bed."

The next day Davy stayed indoors because it was so cold outside. He sat by the window with Nicky, his toy rabbit, waiting for the rest of the family to come home. Davy saw a tiny bird hopping up and down, pecking in the snow.

"Look, Nicky, he's trying to find something to eat," said Davy, "but he won't find anything. The snow is much too deep. Poor little bird."

Davy saw more birds nearby. Their feathers were fluffed up so the birds could stay warm, and they all looked very hungry.

Davy remembered what Father had said last night: "Santa Claus likes us to help one another."

"I'll find some food for the birds," he said.

Davy ran into the pantry and looked around. He saw a big sack of corn. The birds would like that. He lifted the heavy sack down from the shelf and carried it outside.

Davy scattered the corn under the old pine tree,
where the snow wasn't so deep.

"Now the birds will have enough to eat," he said.

As he carried the empty sack back into the burrow,
he saw some deer.

"The poor deer!" said Davy. "How can they find any grass under such deep snow? They need my help, too!" Davy grabbed a bundle of sweet-smelling hay and hauled it over to the edge of the woods.

Davy thought of the other woodland animals. The wild pigs' food lay buried under the snow, and the squirrels were sure to have trouble finding their hidden stores.

Davy filled his little red
hood with apples, carrots, and
acorns, and ran over to the
pine tree once again.

"There!" Davy said to
himself. "Mother and Father
will be so pleased with me
for helping the animals. Santa
Claus will be happy, too!"

He could hardly wait for his
family to come home.

They soon returned to the burrow.

"Hello, Davy," said Mother. "Have you been good?"

Then she noticed that the pantry door was open, and saw the half-empty shelves.

"Davy!" she cried. "Where has our food gone?"

"I-I gave it to the hungry animals," Davy stammered.

"Are you crazy?" shouted Max. "What are we going to eat all winter?"

Davy hadn't thought of that.

He turned to his father.

"You said we should help others, and share things, and love one another. We had so much, and the animals out there had nothing, so I . . ."

Davy's eyes filled with tears.

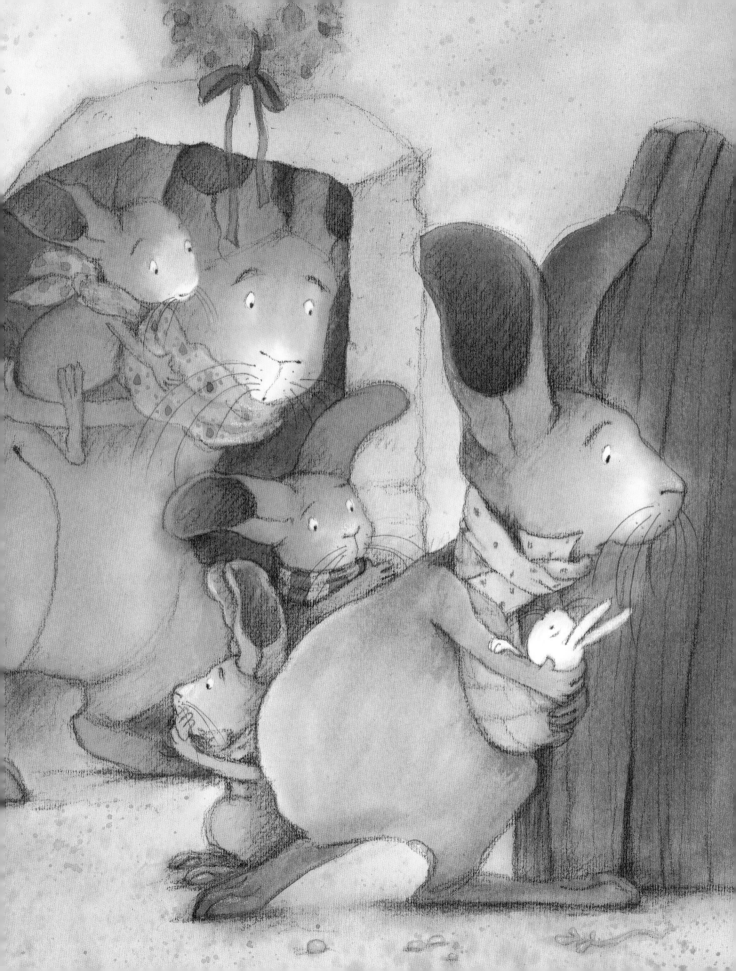

"Wa-a-a!!" wailed Lina. "Davy has given our food away. Now we're going to starve!"

"Mia hungry!" squeaked their baby sister.

And Manni muttered, "What a fool!"

"Don't say that," said Father. "Davy meant well, and he is right. We had a lot, and the other animals had very little, so we shared our food. But don't worry, we won't go hungry."

"That's true," said Mother. "Things could be much worse. If we are careful, our food will last until spring. What's important is that we love and help one another. Will you all promise to do that?"

"We will," they promised.

Time flew by until Christmas. Everyone was very careful not to waste any food. Sometimes Davy didn't even eat all his dinner. He took the last few crumbs over to the pine tree and scattered them on the ground.

He didn't want the animas to think he had forgotten them.

Then it was Christmas Eve. The Rabbits were decorating their Christmas tree when they heard a loud knock on the door. Who could it be?

"It is Santa Claus?" whispered Lina.

Davy certainly hoped it was. He ran to the door.

But when he opened it, he saw birds, deer, squirrels, and
wild pigs standing outside.

One of the birds chirped: "Davy, dear friend. We're so
grateful to you for helping us, and we want to give you a
Christmas present."

He held out a twig, laden with berries. "Next summer we
birds will show you where the sweetest berries grow," he
said, "and you can pick as many as you want."

One of the deer gave Davy a small bundle
of wheat. "We deer will show you fields of
beautiful wheat."

The squirrels had brought some
mushrooms. "We squirrels will show you
where the biggest mushrooms grow,"
they said.

And a wild pig dropped
some carrots and an
apple at Davy's
feet. "We pigs
know where to find
the juiciest apples and
fattest carrots," he grunted.

"Merry Christmas, Davy!" cried all the animals. Then they slipped quietly back into the woods.

"Look what my friends brought!" Davy said to his family.

They carried the gifts inside and laid them under the Christmas tree.

"Mmm, these look delicious," said Davy.

Mother smiled. "Now I have enough apples and berries to bake a Christmas cake," she said.

"Mia hungry!" squeaked the baby.

Davy put a berry in his sister's mouth. "Try this, little Mia," he said. "Next summer you can have lots more. My friends will show us where all the nicest things grow."